For Jeremy and Kathy
J.L.

Text copyright © 1988 by James Latimer
Illustrations copyright © 1988 by Donald Carrick

Charles Scribner's Sons Books for Young Readers
Macmillan Publishing Company · 866 Third Avenue, New York, NY 10022
Collier Macmillan Canada, Inc.

Printed in Japan by Toppan Printing Co.
First Edition   10   9   8   7   6   5   4   3   2   1

Library of Congress Cataloging-in-Publication Data
Latimer, James, 1943–   Going the moose way home.
Summary: A year in the life of a very unusual moose, who shares
his root beer with hungry cows, helps smaller animals across a
troll bridge, and mistakes a train for a lady moose.
[1. Moose—Fiction.   2. Animals—Fiction]
I. Carrick, Donald, ill.   II. Title.
PZ7.L369617Go   1988   [E]   87-9762   ISBN 0-684-18890-2

GOING THE
MOOSE WAY HOME

JIM LATIMER

PICTURES BY
DONALD CARRICK

CHARLES SCRIBNER'S SONS · NEW YORK

Moose is tall, a hill on hoofs and thin stork legs. He has bony shoulders, long ears, soft eyes, a mobile muzzle, and a beard. In fall and winter he has horny antlers—huge toothed blades that rake the sky, that rake the leaves before they fall.

Moose lives in Moosewood, a place of maple trees, wild broccoli, and blueberries, with a post office, an Animal Store, and a county road. In summer Moose likes to walk through marshes to soak his stomach and help digest his food, mainly lily pads and blueberries—and root beer to drink. He is afraid of witches, thunder, and ghosts, but he is not afraid of trolls or wild boars or the dark. On his way home Moose sometimes stands beside the county road to watch for license plates, though he does not know how to read. Once he saw Iowa, Wisconsin, and Rhode Island; he sees a lot of Minnesotas, because he lives in Minnesota, and sometimes Moosechusetts.

Moose would like to walk on walls, but it is hard to walk on walls with hoofs. It is hard to pick blueberries and lily pads, and hard to open bottles, but Moose has a nimble muzzle that can do these things. Moose wishes he could read, but a moose's eyes do not focus the right way.

On his way home Moose almost always passes the Animal Store. The storekeepers, Moose's friends, Newt and Frog, stock Deer brand doughnuts and Blue Jay jam and Wood whipped cream. Also Fox french fries—frozen—and Raccoon rye bread and Bear baked beans. And Moose margarine, Moose mayonnaise, Moose minestrone, Moose marmalade, and Moose molasses.

Moose sometimes makes things up.

Once along the county road, he saw a parade—a marching band. The air was filled with the sound of bells and crackling brass, and there were animal players in the band. There was a frog carrying the flag and a bear playing bells. There was a skunk on spoons and a hare on harp and a porcupine playing pianolin. Moose felt a tingling along his spine. The music was wild and beautiful. It made him want to move in rhythm. It made him want to play a musical instrument. A clarinet. Or maybe maracas.

Along the county road Moose imagines he is a player in a marching band, going His Moose Way Home.

The Marsh

On his way home Moose came to a dark, still pond tiled with green lily pads. Cattails and rushes marched through the pond and around its marshy edges. Ducks and blackbirds crowded the cattails. The pond was perfect, Moose thought. He walked in, parting the lily pads, scattering the birds.

Moose stood a moment, his muzzle quivering, then stretched and delicately plucked a lily pad from the pond. The ducks turned to stare at him. The blackbirds stared. Moose plucked another lily pad and crunched it noisily. It was tender and delicious. He plucked another. Then another.

The ducks, growing cross, scolded and quacked at him. The blackbirds also scolded. But Moose stayed. He stayed all day, growing slick and sleek and fat.

At sunset Moose sighed, rippling the water. He walked out, pulling the pond behind him. The ducks and blackbirds clung to the cattails for dear life. When Moose reached firm ground he let the pond go. He stood a moment with ears dripping, immensely satisfied, then resumed his way. The birds breathed a sigh.

Moose almost took the pond with him, going His Moose Way Home.

Moose and Fox

On his way home Moose stopped at the blueberry bog. Bear was there already, surrounded by high-bush blueberries and looking very fine. Bear's fur sparked and flared, shattering the sunshine like a prism. He was gorgeous and Moose told him so.

"It's because of the wax," Bear said.

Moose blinked at him.

"I got it from Fox," Bear explained.

Moose did not know Fox.

"He's parked along the county road," Bear told him. "He has fur wax and a lot of things. Go and see."

Moose went.

On the county road there was a fox, pushing a peddler's cart. "Good morning," said the fox, hailing Moose with his paw. "Come and look."

Moose couldn't resist.

In the fox's cart there was antler ointment in bottles. There were jars of hoof oil, heather scented. There were bur brushes, coat combs, and tail trimmings. There was fur wax and fur shampoo. Moose peered into the fox's cart, trying to bring the bottles and jars into sharper focus. The fox looked at him shrewdly.

"Look at this," he said. "Today's special. It's Moose Medicine. Just right for your system." Moose did not know what fox meant by his system. "It's your stomach," Fox explained. "Your bones. Your ribs and tonsils. Moose Medicine is wonderful for all of these things."

"I don't have very much money," Moose said. Moose did not have any real money that he knew of.

"Well," said Fox, "maybe you could get some. Do you have a bank?" Moose had a bark bank.

"How much is in your bark bank?" asked Fox.

Moose wasn't sure. It was mostly bark, he thought.

"Well," said Fox, "just bring what you have."

Moose went to get what he had. He brought back bark, two nickels—buffalo nickels—and one Irish penny.

"It's not enough for medicine," said Fox, crestfallen. He thought about it, then brightened. "For two nickels," he said, "you can have your antlers shined." Fox surveyed his bottles and jars. "Shined with shellac," he added. Moose gave Fox his nickels and Fox opened a jar. When he had finished, Moose looked gorgeous, his antlers shellacked and shining.

Moose's antlers looked very fine, going Their Moose Way Home.

Moose and Crow

Once, in winter, Moose walked behind the snowplow along the county road, a safe distance behind. An early snowfall had already risen above his knees in the forest, and he did not want to get stuck.

Moose looked up. Above him the sky was dark and heavy. It grew darker and heavier. The plow, now far ahead, lumbered around a bend in the road and disappeared. Then suddenly the sky seemed to tilt, like the bed of a huge dump truck, and snow dropped down—many, many inches in a very few minutes. Soon the snow had mounted to Moose's stomach, and it did not stop falling. It would have risen to his chin if moose had chins, and rose still higher. When the snow stopped, Moose's muzzle, his ears and eyes and antlers, were all that could be seen of him. On his way home Moose had gotten stuck on the county road, and he stayed stuck.

For a while Moose tried to concentrate, tried to focus on his situation. He thought of the likelihood of the snowplow coming back and finding him. Probably a farmer in a tractor would come and pull him out. But a farmer in a tractor did not come, and the snowplow did not come back, and gradually Moose's mind began to wander.

He thought about Musk Ox, his relative far to the north, about what fine broad hoofs and what a good long coat Musk Ox had. Moose had never appreciated Musk Ox quite as much as he did now. He thought about Musk Ox and many other things. About his calfhood and his wonderful gray-furred mother. About his grandfather, who had fallen in love with a steam engine, mistaking it for a moose. He thought about his first blueberry bog and his first pond of lily pads. Moose thought about trees—about what it was like to *be* a tree, rooted and branching, wandering only in thought. He felt sure he knew what this was like. And Moose thought about a cow, a lovely moose cow. He seemed to see her plunging toward him in the distance, trumpeting a lively greeting.

Moose was wakened from his snow daydream by a noise, a loud cawing somewhere close above him. It was a crow perched in his antlers, and when Moose saw this he was sure he was a tree. He had frozen and died and turned into a tree, and now the crows were roosting in his branches. But the crow spoke to him as a moose.

"You're stuck," Crow said.

Moose admitted he was.

"Don't worry," Crow told him.

Moose wondered why he shouldn't.

"Tomorrow is Monday," Crow explained.

Moose wasn't sure he could follow this.

"The school bus comes on Mondays," Crow continued, "and you are in the way. The plow will come back. It will clear you out of the way."

Moose thought about this.

"You are probably hungry," Crow ventured.

Moose was.

"Don't worry," Crow told him.

Moose wondered why he shouldn't worry.

"The kids on the bus will have lunch boxes. They will give you something," Crow explained. "When the snowplow clears you out," he added.

Moose wondered what clearing out would be like—by a snowplow.

"Don't worry," Crow told him, reading his thoughts. "I have seen animals cleared out before."

"Do you think you could bring me some bark for now?" Moose asked Crow. Crow brought Moose some bark to eat, and they waited for Monday morning together.

On Monday morning the plow, with the school bus following, came back to clear the county road. It cleared quite close to Moose, and he stepped out of the snow. The kids gave Moose and Crow parts of peanut butter sandwiches. Then the moose and the crow, with the school bus and the plow ahead, made a strange parade, going Their Moose Way Home.

Moose and the Troll

On his way home Moose came to a Troll Bridge. A cricket, a muskrat, and an opposum were standing nearby, too frightened to cross, for they knew a terrible troll, fierce and fat, was lurking below. Moose was not afraid of trolls. He told the cricket, the muskrat, and the opposum not to worry, and stepped onto the bridge—and instantly the troll was aware of him.

"What?" the troll shouted. "Another buffalo?" The troll had had a buffalo for breakfast.

Moose said, "No, not a buffalo. I start with *M*," he said.

"A riddle," the troll muttered through stony teeth. "This is a riddle. *Monkey,*" he shouted aloud.

Moose said "No."

"Muskrat," shouted the troll. The muskrat held his breath.

Moose said, "No."

"Mermaid?" the troll asked, becoming a little puzzled.

"No," said Moose.

"A *motorcycle* then," the troll shouted, "or else mistletoe. Or marmalade."

Moose said, "No, no, and no."

"Then you're a magnet." The troll, exasperated, could think of nothing else.

Moose said simply, "I'm a moose."

A *moose,* thought the troll. *Like* a buffalo, he thought, feeling suddenly hungry. The troll came out to look, and there was Moose, a hill on quiet hoofs, seven feet tall and eleven hundred pounds. Moose's antlers, huge toothed shovels, were seventy inches across.

The troll hesitated. He fidgeted, muttering to himself. "I do *not* feel hungry for a moose," he said at last. "You can cross."

Moose crossed the Troll Bridge. Cricket, Muskrat, and Opossum crossed with him—three small animals and one tall animal, going Their Moose Way Home.

Christmas and the Cows

On Christmas morning Moose passed a snowy field along the county road. He didn't quite pass. Twelve black and white cows with steaming breath and sad eyes huddled together close to the fence. The cows stared at Moose, their breath frosting the fur on their foreheads. Moose stared back at them. One of the cows flapped its ears. Then another cow flapped its ears. Moose flapped his ears experimentally, searching for the cows' meaning.

"Hello," he called to them, but the cows did not answer. They stood, steaming and staring, ears flapping, looking very sad.

"Merry Christmas," Moose called. The cows did not wish Moose a Merry Christmas.

"Happy Chanukah," he said, though Chanukah was almost two weeks past. The cows did not answer him.

Moose stood quietly, not wishing to walk away. They are sad, he thought. He saw the cows did not have grass to eat. The grass lay asleep under a blanket of heavy snow, and there was no hay. The cows' eyes were more sad than any eyes Moose had ever seen. Now I am sad, he thought.

Moose wondered what the cows would like. He had blueberries, frozen, and lily pads and bark, and root beer in bottles—twelve green bottles of dark root beer. Moose hurried home and hurried back again with lily pads—with lily pads and blueberries and bark and root beer for the cows.

The cows tried all of these things. They did not like frozen blueberries. They did not like bark or root beer in bottles. But they liked lily pads.

On Christmas morning Moose ate tender, green lily pads with twelve black and white cows, going His Moose Way Home.

Valentine's Day

On Saint Valentine's Day Moose saw something sleek and steaming, a great, sleek engine moving through the forest. A train had not come through Moosewood for many years. Moose sniffed, his ears and eyes alert. He squinted, trying to bring the thing into focus. "It is a moose," he said. "A moose cow." Moose peered at the train, which was still quite far away. It was the cow from his dream, the lovely cow he had dreamed of while he was stuck in the snow. Moose trembled with excitement. The cow's breath plumed above her head in graceful puffs. Her eyes were like lamps, beautiful, and she moved in rhythm, with great strong strides. Then Moose's eyes grew wide. The cow was moving toward him, in his direction. And then she called to him.

At first quavery and quiet, the cow's call rose to a strong, steamy moo. The cow was calling *him*, Moose. She was calling to him on Valentine's Day.

Moose barked. He capered. He frisked and capered and leaped about, calling back to the cow, and then he ran home.

Moose came back very soon with a velvet ribbon, a valentine for the beautiful cow. But—Moose peered, squinting, into the distance—the train had gone. *She* had gone. The lovely cow had not waited for him.

Moose grew still. He thought he could hear a quavery whistle, now far away. He waited, but the cow did not come back.

On his way home Moose's heart felt heavy. His head was down, his ears drooping. He saw his friend Skunk standing beside a bush, looking low.

"What?" Moose asked her. "Why are you sad?"

"Because," Skunk told him, "nobody has asked me to be his valentine. Nobody ever does," she said. "Valentine's Day is my worst day. It is my worst day of the year."

Moose thought about this. He liked Skunk, though he had not asked her to be his valentine. He never had.

"No one ever asks you?" Moose asked her.

Skunk shook her head. "No one wants a skunk for a valentine," she said.

"I do," Moose told her.

On his way home Moose asked Skunk to be his valentine, and Skunk said, "Yes."

The Easter Rabbit

On his way home one morning Moose saw a rabbit sitting beside a bush. The rabbit had a worried look. Beside him there was a covered basket, a hamper with handles and leather carrying straps. In the rabbit's lap lay a pencil and a folded paper. The rabbit looked up at Moose with alarm.

"Good morning," Moose ventured.

"*Easter* morning," the rabbit corrected. "And *not* very good," he said.

It *was* Easter morning, Moose remembered, though he could not think why it wouldn't be good.

"Because I forgot to deliver my eggs," the rabbit explained.

Moose's eyes widened. He looked at the rabbit's hamper. Forgot to deliver his *eggs*? Could this be the Easter Rabbit? "How do you mean?" Moose asked aloud. "How do you mean 'forgot'?"

"I was working a crossword puzzle," the rabbit said, pointing to the paper. "It was a good one—a good hard one," he added. "And now I am in trouble."

Moose thought this over. He had heard of crossword puzzles, but he had never met an animal who knew how to work them. "Are you the Easter Rabbit?" he asked.

"I'm *an* Easter Rabbit. The Easter Rabbit for this district. And when the Head Easter Rabbit finds out about this, I am going to be in trouble."

What will the Head Easter Rabbit do? Moose wanted to ask. But instead he said, "Wait, I'll be back," and galloped away, calling to the rabbit to get his eggs ready.

Moose ran to get his friend Skunk. When he got back, the three of them, Skunk, Moose, and Rabbit, set out for Opossum's, the first house on Rabbit's list.

Opossum looked very gloomy when they found her. "What?" Skunk asked. "What's the matter?" The Easter Rabbit hid behind Moose.

"It's Easter morning," Opossum said, "and I did not get any eggs—not one."

"Well, have you looked?" Skunk asked her.

"Everywhere," said Opossum.

"Where?" asked Moose.

"Under my bed," said Opossum. "In my sewing drawer. In my refrigerator. On the windowsill. On top of the doorway. Under the kitchen table. In the pantry. Usually Rabbit puts the eggs in easy places."

"Have you looked in your coat pockets?" Skunk asked her. Opossum had not looked in her coat pockets.

"Have you looked in your pajamas?" Moose asked. Opossum had not looked in her pajamas. Or under her radiator. Or on top of her piano. Or behind her blender.

While Opossum was looking behind her blender, Rabbit hid three beautiful Easter eggs in her pajamas. While Porcupine was looking through *his* pajamas, Rabbit hid three eggs under his radiator. While Newt was looking through his coat pockets, Rabbit hid three Easter eggs on top of his piano.

In this way, Skunk, Moose, and Rabbit delivered all the eggs in Rabbit's hamper, a little late on Easter morning, going Their Moose Way Home. And Rabbit did not get into trouble.

Moose's Birthday

Moose liked cake. He had never had one, but he liked the *idea* of cake. He would make a cake for his birthday, a blueberry birthday cake—maybe blueberry and buttermilk. Maybe *root beer* and buttermilk.

On his birthday Moose bought root beer, four bottles, and buttermilk for batter—for his cake. He slung a cloth bag over his shoulder with the four bottles of root beer inside (three for the batter and one to drink) and two half-pints of buttermilk.

On his way home he came to the Troll Bridge. The troll, instantly aware of him, shouted, *"Who is it?"*

"It's Moose," said Moose.

The troll came out to see. "What's that bag?" he demanded.

"It's a bag," Moose told him. "With root beer and buttermilk."

The troll did not like buttermilk, but he loved root beer. "I love root beer," he shouted at Moose. "I would love a bottle of root beer."

Moose brought out a bottle of root beer for the troll.

"*Two* bottles," the troll demanded.

Moose gave two bottles to the troll and resumed his way.

Across the bridge, two sheep were grazing. The sheep lifted their heads when they saw Moose. "What's in your bag?" they asked him.

"Root beer," Moose answered. "And buttermilk for batter. For a cake."

"I love buttermilk," said one sheep.

"I have not had any root beer for a long time," said the other.

Moose gave the sheep a bottle of root beer and one half-pint of buttermilk and resumed his way, until he came to sixteen squirrels.

The squirrels were beautifully dressed, but they were crying. "What's the matter?" Moose asked them.

"It's a wedding," said one of the squirrels, pointing to the bride and groom, "but we do not have anything to celebrate with—only nuts."

"Well, how about buttermilk?" Moose asked them. The squirrels stopped crying. Moose gave them his last half-pint of buttermilk and a bottle of root beer, his last, and resumed his way.

Now *he* did not have anything to celebrate with. Moose had given away the ingredients for his birthday cake.

On his way home Moose saw Skunk standing beside a bush, looking worried.

"What?" he asked her. "What's the matter?"

"I am looking for you," Skunk told him. There was worry in her voice. "Newt and Frog are locked out," she said.

"Locked out?" Moose asked her.

"Locked out of the store," Skunk explained. "The door is locked shut and they are outside," she said. "They need an animal with strong hoofs— to open the door for them."

Moose brightened. His hoofs were strong. His *kick* was strong. If he had had a ball, he might have kicked it the length of the county road—maybe all the way to Canada. He would open Newt and Frog's door, he said, but when Moose and Skunk arrived at the Animal Store the door was not locked shut. It was wide open, and inside were Newt and Frog, Crow and Bear, Cricket and Opossum and Raccoon. They had come to celebrate Moose's birthday—with cake. Root beer and buttermilk cake. With blueberries and lily pads on the side.

When Moose's friends had finished their cake (three huge wedges for each one), they asked him to tell his birthday wish.

Moose thought about it. The cake was his wish, he told them, and now it had come true.

"Wish for something else," Skunk told him. "On your birthday you should wish for something that is not true—something that has not *come* true," she said, and Newt and Frog agreed.

"Something more special than cake," they said.

Moose thought about this, and at last he thought of a wish more special than birthday cake.

"I wish I could read," he said. "I wish I could read *music*."

Moose said he would play a musical instrument, a piano or a clarinet. Maybe maracas. He would play in a parade, marching along the county road.

Moose's friends clapped for his birthday wish, going Their Moose Way Home.

On his way home along the county road, Moose saw a parade—a marching band. The air was filled with the sound of crackling brass and bells, and there were animal players in the band. Frog was carrying the flag and Bear was playing bells. There was Skunk on spoons and Crow on clarinet. And Moose—on maracas? No, and a *Moose Major*.

Moose dreamed he was a major in a marching band, going His Moose Way Home.